DANNY BROWN
AND HIS
DAFT
DOG

THE O'BRIEN PRESS
DUBLIN

For Kevin –
Danny's first fan,
with love and thanks.

This edition first published 2018 by

The O'Brien Press Ltd.

12 Terenure Road East, Rathgar,

Dublin 6, D06 HD27, Ireland.

Tel: +353 1 492 3333; Fax: +353 1 492 2777

Email: books@obrien.ie

Website: www.obrien.ie

Originally published as *Danny's Pesky Pet*, part of the O'Brien Panda series 2003.

Reprinted 2006, 2008, 2015.

The O'Brien Press is a member of Publishing Ireland.

ISBN: 978-1-78849-011-5

8 7 6 5 4 3 2 1

22 21 20 19 18

Printed and bound by Białostockie Zakłady Graficzne S.A.

The paper in this book is produced using pulp from managed forests.

Published in:

DUBLIN
UNESCO
City of Literature

Danny Brown strikes again ...

Danny was in a big hurry.

He grabbed his warm coat.

He put the lead on Keeno.

'Let's go, Grandpa,' he said.

'I'm ready.'

You're so slow, Grandpa!

'Just a minute!' said Mum.
'It's cold. Susie will need her hat.
The woolly one with the
big pink bobble.'

Danny didn't want
Susie to come.
He whispered to Grandpa:
'Susie can stay at home.
It's too cold for babies.'

Grandpa smiled.

'It's cold for animals, too,'
he said.

'Some animals die
from the cold.
And Keeno has no hat!
Maybe we should leave
Keeno at home.'

'No way!' said Danny.

Danny and Grandpa
walked to the park.
'Walk quickly, Danny,'
said Grandpa. 'It will
help you to keep warm.'

'Come on, Keeno!'
called Danny.
'Hurry up or you'll die
from the cold.'

'Grandpa,' asked Danny,
'how do animals keep warm
in winter?'

'Some animals grow
thick woolly coats,'
said Grandpa.

Poor Keeno has no coat,
thought Danny.

'And hedgehogs hibernate,'
added Grandpa.
'Do you know
what that means, Danny?'

Danny wasn't sure.

'Of course I do!' he said.

'It means they go **hyper**.'

Grandpa laughed out loud.
'Ho! Ho! Ho!'

'No, Danny,' he said.
'It means they go for
a long winter sleep.'

Suddenly a small, grey squirrel
darted along the ground.
'Look,' whispered Grandpa.
'That squirrel is gathering nuts.
Squirrels collect lots of nuts
for the cold winter days.'

Hey! I'm not a nut!

'That's very clever,' said Danny.

Soon they came to the lake.
The water was frozen.
Grandpa took some bread
out of his pocket.
'Let's feed the ducks,'
he said.

Danny stared at the ducks.
They slid along the ice.
'Their little bottoms
must be **frozen**,' he said.

Susie watched Grandpa
throw bread to the ducks.
'Quack! Quack! Quack!'
she said.
The bobble on her hat
bobbed up and down.

Keeno stood by the edge
of the lake and shivered.
Danny looked at Susie's hat.
Keeno needs a hat, he thought.

Then he had a great idea.

He grabbed Susie's woolly hat.
'Keeno!' whispered Danny.
'Come here, boy!'

Keeno ran to Danny.

Danny put Susie's woolly hat
on Keeno's head.
'Woof!' barked Keeno.

'**Waaaaaaaaaaaaaah**!'
cried Susie.
Oh no! thought Danny.
What will I do?

Danny could see bread in
Grandpa's pocket.
He pulled out
some of the bread.
'Here, Susie,' he whispered.

But Keeno snatched the bread.
He raced around the park.
He barked and jumped.
Susie's hat went flying
up into a tree.

Grandpa laughed till he shook.
Then he got a stick and hit
Susie's hat down.
It fell in the mud.

'Oh, Danny!' said Grandpa.
'I think we're in trouble!'

Oh no!
More trouble!

But when they got home
nobody saw the dirty hat.

Granny was complaining.

'It's so cold!' she grumbled.

She was wearing her

big blue cardigan.

She pulled it tightly around her.

Danny thought Granny
looked like a
huge hedgehog.
'Why don't you hibernate,
Granny?' he asked.

A whole
winter
without
Granny!
Yippee!

Mum laughed.

'Try these first,' she said.

She held up two

big pink woolly socks.

'They're bedsocks,'

she explained.

'Wonderful!' Granny said.
'Every night my feet are like
two lumps of ice!'

Danny had an idea.

'Mum,' he said. 'Keeno needs
warm woollies too.

Will you knit something
for him?'

'Are you crazy?' cried Mum.
'Dogs don't need woollies!'
And Mum walked off
without another word.

Danny was very cross.

He saw Susie's hat on the table.

He took the hat

and put it on Keeno's head.

Susie's gloves were on a chair.

Danny took the gloves

and put them on

Keeno's front paws.

'You need something
for your back paws too, Keeno,'
said Danny.
'They might turn to ice
like Granny's feet!'

Suddenly Danny
had a great idea.
'I know what you can wear!
Granny's bedsocks!
They'll do the trick!'
Danny put Granny's bedsocks
on Keeno.

Keeno yawned –
a big, long yawn.
'Keeno!' cried Danny excitedly.
'You should hibernate
like the hedgehog.'

Lovely warm dog!

Then Danny thought
of the clever squirrel
with his pile of nuts.
'And you should have
lots of food like the squirrel,'
he said.

He went to a cupboard.
It was full of tins of dog food.

Danny opened lots of tins.
He gathered them up
in his arms.

'Now, let's find somewhere
for you to hibernate!' he said.

Keeno followed Danny upstairs.

The spare bedroom was empty.

'This is perfect, Keeno!'

whispered Danny.

Danny left the dog food
on the floor.
He put Keeno in
one of the beds.
'Now, go to sleep, Keeno!'
he said.

Everyone was
watching television
when Danny came downstairs.

'The weather forecast is
very bad,' said Grandpa.
'Icy roads tonight!'

'We'll have to drive carefully,'
Granny warned.
'We don't want to have
an accident.'

But Mum had a better idea.
'You should stay here!
You can sleep
in the spare bedroom!'

Grandpa looked at Granny.
'That would be
much safer,' he said.
'And you've got your
warm woolly bedsocks
for the night!
You'll be snug as a bug.'

Danny was shocked.
Oh no! he thought.
He darted upstairs.

'Keeno! Keeno!' called Danny.
'It's time to get up!'

Danny went into
the spare bedroom.

The tins of food were scattered
all over the floor.
The quilt was a mess.
Keeno was covered in dogfood.
And he was chewing
Granny's bedsocks!

'**Oh no**!' cried Danny.

Just then, Danny heard Granny
coming up the stairs.
'Goodnight, everyone!'
she called.

Danny ran to
the bedroom door.
He held out his arms.
'No, Granny!' he yelled.
'**No**! **No**! **No**!
You can't go in there.'

Mum and Grandpa
hurried up the stairs.
'What's the matter?'
said Mum.

'Granny can't go **in there**!'
yelled Danny.

'Why not?' asked Grandpa.

'It's ... It's **too cold** in there!' cried Danny.

'Her feet will turn into two lumps of ice!'

Put Granny in the shed!

'I'll get her **new bedsocks**!' said Grandpa.

Granny lifted Danny
out of her way.
She opened the door
and went in.

'Woof! Woof!' barked Keeno.
Granny stopped.
'Good heavens!' she shrieked.

Mum and Grandpa ran in.
'What's wrong?' asked Mum.

Danny peeped in at them.

Granny was standing
beside the bed.
Her feet were covered
in dogfood.
She was pulling her
new bedsocks out of
Keeno's mouth.

Keeno was very excited.
'Woof! Woof!' he barked.
He jumped at Granny,
then he lifted his leg and
wet Granny's feet!

'**Danny**!' yelled Mum.
'**Danny**!' screeched Granny.

'Danny,' whispered Grandpa.
He opened Danny's
bedroom door.
'Quick! In here, Danny!'
he said. 'I think it's time
for **you** to hibernate!'

Danny jumped
into his own bed.
He was in **big trouble**!

He covered his head
with the quilt.

'I'll never do anything
like this again,' he said.
'Never. Never. Never.'

BUT I THINK HE WILL, DON'T YOU?
DANNY'S JUST THAT KIND OF KID.